Marta Mouse and Willy Weasel
are building a raft. What will
they find to build it with?

Celia Swan is looking for a new house for her children.
Sippi, the youngest, is very mischievous.
Can you see what kind of trouble he gets into?
And where will they make their home?

Old Mr. Goat is taking his dog,
Dexter, for a walk. Dexter is very curious.
What will Dexter find along the way?

The Road Hogs are having a race.
But why are they in such a hurry?

Chuck the Chicken loves to roller-skate.
He also loves to help his friends.
Who will he help along the way?

The Party Animals love to dance
and make music. They just want to have fun.
Do you want to join their party?

Laura Lamb has terribly bad luck fishing.
Can you see what she catches?

Mama and Papa can make themselves at
home anywhere. Where would you like to live?

Magnus Weightman

All Along
the River

Clavis

NEW YORK

High up above the clouds, all is quiet.
The only sound is the creaking of the glacier.
Bunny is playing happily near the water.
"Help!" she suddenly shouts. "Peter! Bob! Little Duck
is floating away!" Her brothers jump straight into their boat.
"Quick! Let's catch her before she's gone forever!"

Down the stream, deep into the forest they go.
"Have you seen a small duck float by?" they call to the Fox family.
But who could ever find Little Duck in this fast, bubbly water?

The water slows down as it twists
and turns its way through the green valley.
"Mr. Farmer, have you seen a little yellow duck come by?"
He shakes his head. Maybe the horses have seen her,
or the cows, perhaps?

The river opens up and stretches out as far as the eye can see.
"Oh, my Little Duck. How will we ever find you on this huge lake?"
asks a worried Bunny. Could she be there on the beach, or between
the sailing boats? Or has Freddy Fox spotted her in the reeds?

What's that roar? Why are they speeding up?
Oh no, a waterfall! Hold on tight, bunnies!
But where could Little Duck be in this mighty cloud of water?

It's party time in town. "Look there, next to the toy boat! Is that Little Duck?" calls Bunny as she jumps into the water. Or is she by the unicorn? Or the raft?

The river meanders and takes the boat by a factory. *Has Little Duck been swallowed up by one of these steel monsters?* Bunny wonders. They search high and low, but Little Duck is nowhere to be seen. Or is she?

It has started to rain. Wow, what a beautiful maze of water and islands.
"Dear swans, can you help us please? We've lost our toy duck," calls Bunny.
"Sorry, we haven't seen her . . ." answers Celia Swan.

"Help! Our ball has fallen in the water!" shout the soccer players from the side.
The bunnies rescue the ball, but they still haven't found Little Duck.
Where could she be among all these amazing tulips?

The rabbits arrive in the harbor. What a busy place!
"Look out!" cries Bunny as a container of rubber ducks spills into the water.
"Oh no, how will I find my Little Duck now?" But there's only one Little Duck, right?

The waves wash up on the seashore. Bunny climbs the lighthouse to have a look and shouts, "Yes, I can see her!" And there she is, floating out to sea. Quick, bunnies - there is no time to lose!

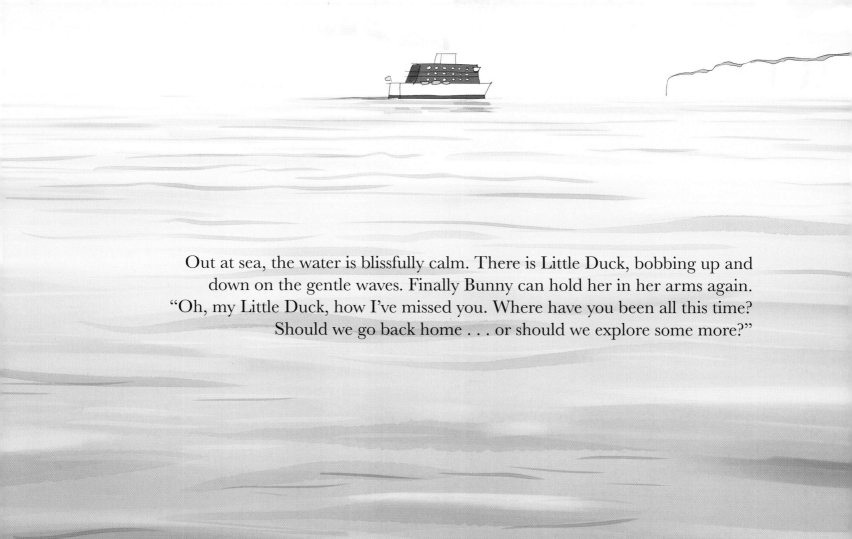

Out at sea, the water is blissfully calm. There is Little Duck, bobbing up and down on the gentle waves. Finally Bunny can hold her in her arms again. "Oh, my Little Duck, how I've missed you. Where have you been all this time? Should we go back home . . . or should we explore some more?"

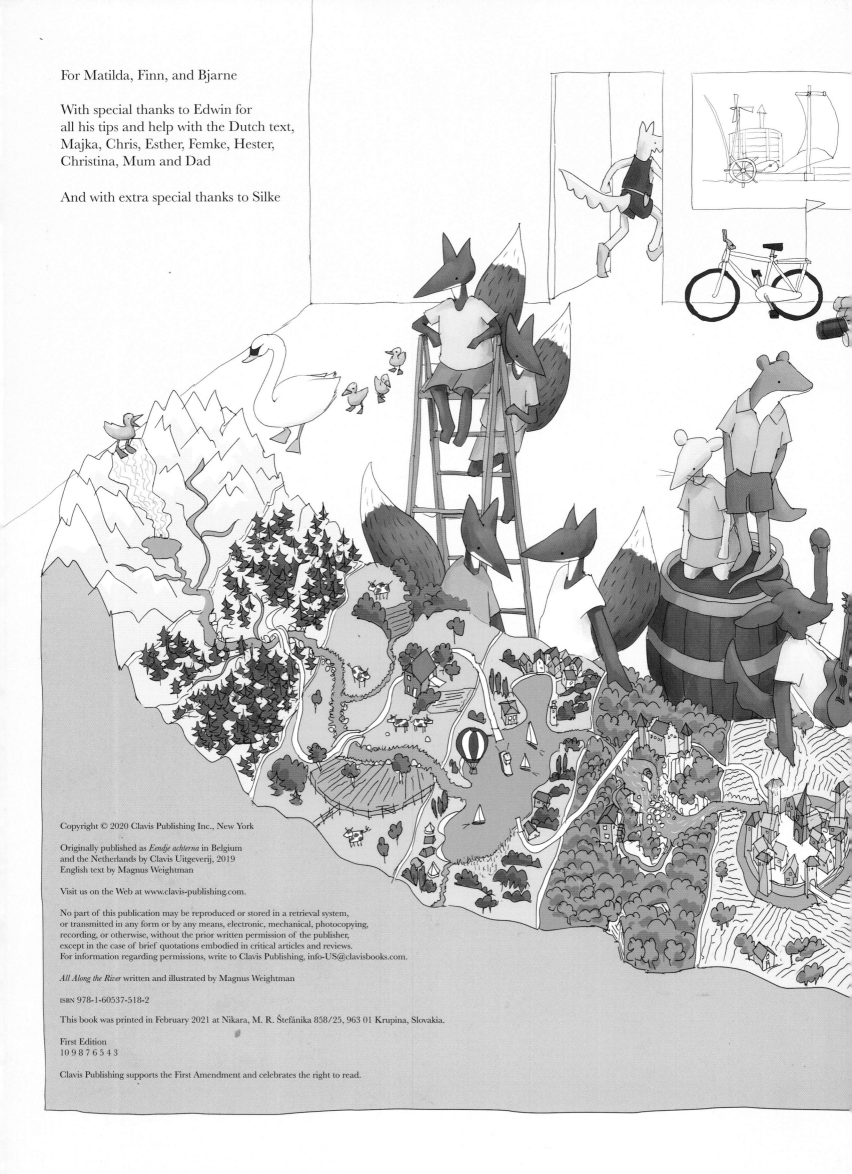

For Matilda, Finn, and Bjarne

With special thanks to Edwin for
all his tips and help with the Dutch text,
Majka, Chris, Esther, Femke, Hester,
Christina, Mum and Dad

And with extra special thanks to Silke

Originally published as *Eendje achterna* in Belgium
and the Netherlands by Clavis Uitgeverij, 2019
English text by Magnus Weightman

Visit us on the Web at www.clavis-publishing.com.

All Along the River written and illustrated by Magnus Weightman

ISBN 978-1-60537-518-2

This book was printed in February 2021 at Nikara, M. R. Štefánika 858/25, 963 01 Krupina, Slovakia.

First Edition
10 9 8 7 6 5 4 3